All Families Are Special

Norma Simon

ILLUSTRATED BY Teresa Flavin

Albert Whitman & Company
Morton Grove, Illinois

This book is for the Storytellers of Wellfleet Elementary School and
for Dr. Maggie Mack. We shared and learned so much from each other.
N.S.

For Pablo.
T.F.

Library of Congress Cataloging-in-Publication Data

Simon, Norma.
All families are special / by Norma Simon ; illustrated by Teresa Flavin.
p. cm.
Summary: Students in Mrs. Mack's class describe their families—big or small, living together or apart,
with two moms or none—and learn why every family is special and important.
ISBN 0-8075-2175-2 (hardcover)
[1. Family—Fiction. 2. Schools—Fiction.] I. Flavin, Teresa, ill. II. Title.
PZ7.S6053Al 2003 [E]—dc21 2003002094

The illustrations were done in watercolor.
The design is by Carol Gildar.

For more information about Albert Whitman & Company,
please visit our web site at www.albertwhitman.com.

ABOUT THIS BOOK

We remain linked to our families, and to our family memories, throughout our lives. That's because of the powerful emotional bonds formed in family life.

Kinship plays a significant role in shaping the personality and self-image of every child in a family. The strengths children develop and the successes they experience within their families shape the strengths and expectations of success they carry with them as they grow up and move out into the world. The family environment influences how children thrive and mature; eventually it influences their ability to form happy families of their own.

We know that nobody lives a perfect life. Family life includes times of tension and hardship as well as times of great joy. It is up to adult family members to create a climate of love, security and optimism that will help children weather stormy times and find life's most positive values and experiences.

The typical family picture of fifty years ago has undergone many changes. Today's children live in two-parent families, single-parent families, adoptive families, foster families, divorced families, and blended families. This book invites children to describe their own family group, and, through these discussions, to realize and appreciate all the ways their families are special, *very special*.

Norma Simon

Do you know what I found out today?
Mrs. Mack, my teacher, is going to be a grandma!
She told our class, "My daughter is having a baby.
I'll be the baby's grandmother. I can hardly wait!"

All the kids were surprised.
It's funny to think that teachers have families.
"Everyone is part of a family," Mrs. Mack said.
"Would you like to talk about *your* families?"
Hands shot up all over the room.

Mrs. Mack said, "Sarah, you begin."

"Well," said Sarah, "there are four of us in my family.

There's my mom and dad and me, and my little sister, Rachel.

She's four years old.

We adopted her from China when she was almost a year old.

Mom and Dad and I flew to China, over a huge ocean,

miles and miles and miles away, to bring Rachel home.

"On the long plane ride home,
Rachel walked up and down the aisle with me,
holding onto my hands.
Everybody smiled at us.
We loved Rachel right away."

Nick was waving his hand.

"Let's see—there's Mama and Papa.

There's Grandma and Grandpa.

We have a new baby, Josh.

I have two big sisters and two little brothers.

Me—I'm right in the middle.

That makes ten people, in one house!

When my family orders pizzas,

we need three super ones!"

"Ten people—that's one big family!" Mrs. Mack said.
"Families come in all sizes, don't they?
Who has a small family?"

Matt raised his hand.

"My family is only two people, my dad and me.

My mom died when I was two years old.

We have lots of pictures of her.

I like the wedding pictures best—

she looks so beautiful in her long white dress!

There's one of Mom and me that I like, too."

Hannah, who's never shy, wanted her turn.

"I have two mommies, Michelle and Annie.

In our family, we all ride bikes, take hikes, and go camping.

Michelle and Annie both have green thumbs.

That means they know how to grow flowers and vegetables.

I'm a good gardener, too."

Grace was next.
"Our family has three people,"
she said. "Mom, Dad and me.
But my dad has to travel for his work,
so lots of times it's just Mom and me at home.
I wish he had a different job.

"When my dad is someplace far away, he calls
us before I go to sleep. He says, 'I miss you!'
Some nights he tells me something funny
that happened, and we both laugh."

Then Jessica told about her family.

"Harry lives with us—my mom, my brother, and me.

Harry's just like my dad, but he's not our real father.

My real father moved away when I was still a baby, so I never knew him.

My brother says he remembers him a little.

"But Harry's great. He taught me how to pitch,

and he helps me with my math.

We like a lot of the same books and movies.

Yeah, I really like Harry."

It was Juan's turn.

"My family is medium size, I guess.

There's Mom and Dad, and us kids. We moved into Grandma's house when she came home from the hospital.

Grandma is much better now, but she still needs us to help her.

I love Grandma's old house. It has a big porch and big backyard.

Dad lived there when he was growing up.

Let's see—Grandma, Mom, Dad, me, my twin sisters, Jennie and Carla—that makes six people in my family."

Next, it was Salma's turn.

"My family lives in two places," she explained.

"Grandma and Grandpa live in Pakistan.

Mom and Dad were born there. They came to the United States

when my brother was just a baby. I was born here.

"Grandpa and Grandma come to visit us every year.

Grandma shows me how to make Pakistani foods, like samosas.

Grandpa goes to watch my brother's Little League games.

I wish they would stay in America,

but they say they're too old

to leave their home for good.

We all cry a little when they go.

Then we can't wait until they

come next time!"

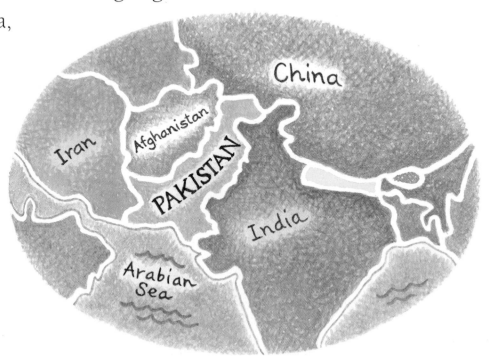

Next, it was my turn.

"There's me, my mom, my dad, my sister, and my brother.

There's our dog, Callie, too.

We used to have a cat—Mama Cat—but she died last summer.

Is it okay to say a cat and dog are part of your family, Mrs. Mack?"

"Sure, Robert," Mrs. Mack said.

"Well, everyone in my family misses Mama Cat, even Callie," I said.

Kevin told us, "I live with Grandpa, Grandma—and Mom, just on weekends.
When Mom comes, she sleeps in the bottom bunk bed in my room.
It used to be her room, when she was growing up.
I love it when I wake up and she's there.

"I have lots of aunts, uncles, and cousins, too.
When the whole family gets together, like on Thanksgiving,
it's one big bunch of people!
The day after Thanksgiving, I always go to the movies
with all my cousins."

"In my family," Christopher told us, "my mom and dad got divorced.
My dad moved to an apartment, but we still live in our old house with Mom.
My big brother and I keep most of our things in our house, with Mom.

"But we have stuff at Dad's apartment, too.
We're usually over there a couple of days a week.
That's the way it is when you divorce."

Emily raised her hand,
"I have two families, too," she said.
"My mom and dad are divorced.
Then last year, Dad got married again, to Karen.
She's not my mom, but she's really nice.
She's my stepmom.

"Karen's kids are my stepbrother and stepsister.
It took a long time until we all got used to living together.
Now Mom is going to marry her boyfriend, Tom.
Tom's daughter, Maria, visits us on weekends.
We have a good time together."

After everyone had a turn,
Mrs. Mack said,
"Part of living in a family is
sharing happy times and sad times.
Can you think of some unhappy things
that happen in families?"

Lots of hands went up.
The kids talked about when somebody gets sick, and the doctor says, "It's serious."
Or when a mom loses her job and she can't find a new one.
Or when a mom and dad argue all the time, and they decide to get a divorce.
The children feel pulled, back and forth, between them.

When we talked about good things that happen in families,
everybody had lots to tell —

about sending pictures to Grandpa and
Grandma to put on the refrigerator door,

about our family picnics,
sending e-mail to cousins,

going to stay with relatives
who live far away,

building a neat treehouse
with a favorite uncle,
feeling happy when everyone
gets together on holidays.

Mrs. Mack told us,
"When there are bad times,
families help each other to feel better.

"When there are good times,
families enjoy them together.

"The different people in our families
all fit together, like pieces in a puzzle.
You are a *very* important piece of the picture!

"No families are the same.
All families are *definitely* special!"